Foreword

This is my third foray into the world of published writing.
It is in part a continuation from my first effort.

Part one is again written with credit to the work of Diana Gabaldon
and the Outlander TV series.
The characters are of her invention, and the work is Intended as
parody and also as tribute to the masterful characters she has
created.

Part 2 is some of my work written during a traumatic period in my
own life in 2019, and also during pandemic lockdown in Wales
during the Summer of 2020 and the events of the time.

All revenue generated by this book will be donated to
Riding for the Disabled.

Again thanks to the Outlander fan pages of which I am a member for
not getting bored, and for suggesting subject matter, correcting
spelling, and accuracy, a source of constructive and welcome
criticism and again pushing me out of my comfort zone and urging
me to publish.

Hope you enjoy

D1711027

Table of Contents

A Hot Bath	4
A Woman Scorned	5
Claire	7
Angus Mhor	9
Rupert Thomas Alexander Mackenzie	11
Cranesmuir	12
Drama in the Hall	14
Fixing the Mill	16
Master Raymond	18
Parisian to the Core	20
Redcoats	22
The Laird and his Wife	23
The Bonnie Prince	25
Wedding Planning	26
Second Time Around	28
A Back Wood Man from Wales	30
Family, Waifs and Strays	31
Palmistry	33
The Privy Counsel!	34
The First Visit	36
Life at Ardsmuir	38
Thoughts in Print	40
Finding Jamie	43
A Man of Letters	46
Jenny Murray	48
The Full Scottish	50
A Snake in the Grass	52
Burying Hayes	55
Robbed	57
Kidnapped	60

Goats and Hell	62
The White Sow	65
Jamie's Birthday Checklist	67
Introduction to Part 2	68
Watching the Rugby (Wales v Scotland)	69
Domestic Update	71
Turning Leaves	73
Flashback	75
Gone Missing	76
Black Lives Matter	78
Lockdown Revisited	80
Statues and Statutes	81
When your you isn't you anymore	83
Turning Corners	85
Circles	87
Walking Home from Nights	89
Dunraven Bay	90
Turning Out	91
American Scrapbook	92
Parents	94
The Clock in the Hall	96
The Authors Dream.	99

A Hot Bath

A cave beneath the monastery
Dark as blessed night,
A hot spring fills a pitch black lake.
Stars provide the only light.

I floated in the darkness,
Feeling my self heal,
Warmth invaded all my scars
I began once more to feel.

Water washed right through my soul
I felt the pain depart.
Maybe it could heal us both
Of sorrows to our hearts.

I thought of all she'd said and done,
Her selfless act of courage,
Her desperate plea that she could heal
My mind and then our marriage.

I will bring her to this sacred place.
Hold her in my arms,
Let the water do it's work,
Let the heat work all it's charms.

We need to find connection,
We need to find a path,
And I know what she misses most.
Claire loves a good hot bath.

****

4

A Woman Scorned

Jamie Fraser came to live
At Leoch when I was seven,
I told myself I loved him,
To me he looked like heaven.

Then I thought I'd marry him
But he went away.
When he returned
I knew that he was mine, from that very day.

I'd whiled away the hours,
While I did the chores
Imagining that he was mine.
And the other women, whores.

I told myself small stories
Of imagined married life.
He was Laird of Lallybroch
And I was his wife.

I fantasised and romanced,
Convinced myself twas true.
And when he took my punishment
I knew what I must do.

I made myself available,
I sat where he could see,
But he had eyes only for her
He didn't look at me.

Yes, I let him kiss me
I tried to turn his head
But when the English whore looked at him
I'd just as well be dead.

Cold English whore,
I hated you, even from the start
Jamie Fraser will be mine
You will never have his heart.

And in the end I got him
But life was not all honey.
All I really wanted,
From my Jamie, was his money.

****

Claire

Brought up by my Uncle Lamb,
Most unusual for the day.
We travelled and I learned of life
I learned to make my own way.

A streak of independence,
That wouldn't yet conform.
A drive to do things with my life
Not live it in the norm.

A marriage during wartime
Is hard to keep together.
Not seeing him for many years
Made it heavy weather.

And I saw more of war than him,
He was behind the scenes.
I saw the bodies and the blood
It's me who has those dreams.

Frank was my first love,
But not one to the end.
After the war, when he came back
He was more like a friend.

For the sake of continuity
We tacked us back together
Tried to start where we left off.
It would never last forever.

I didn't mean to fall for him
Fall through the veil of time,
A thing bigger than both of us
Meant him to be mine.

We know each other's inner thoughts,
Read each other's mind.
Know when each is feeling pain
Know which wounds to bind.

Death can never cut the cord
The bond death cannot sever
Blood of blood, bone of bone,
I'm bound to you forever.

****

Angus Mhor

Angus Mhor – Big Angus
But on TV I'm not large.
I'm kind of like a terrier.
I growl a lot, then charge.

I'm a Clansman, a Mackenzie
And with my wingman Rupert
We live at Castle Leoch
And travel round with Dougal.

If I want a fight, I'll start one
I'm an expert with a knife.
I wasn't really fussed on Claire,
When she became Jamie's wife.

She's not like Scottish women,
She'll no do as she's told,
She'll get in serious trouble here
Before she gets too old.

Jamie's got his hands full
With his feisty English wife.
If he doesna get a grip on her.
He may just lose his life.

He needs to have a wee word,
Remind her of her place.
To rescue her is not our job.
We've enough upon our plates.

Sort yer wife out Jamie,
In the Scottish way
Spare the strap and spoil the wife.
Dougals' men would say.

****

Rupert Thomas Alexander Mackenzie

Dougal had a choice ye ken
She coulda married me.
Yon red haird loon coulda said no
To the bride to be.

But I dinna think she'd gang fer me
I'm really no her thing,
A bit more rough and ready – ye ken.
Than the lad that bought the ring.

He'd already gone all gooey eed
Since when she fixed his arm.
She's handy with the stitches ay
And she doesna try to harm.

She does all that by accident,
She doesna have tae try
Keepin them safe's a full time job
But ye ken that by and by.

So me and my wee Angus
May chaff her – here and there.
But we'd both lay our lives down.
For Jamie and for Claire

****

Cranesmuir

Jamie warned me not to,
But I had to go.
The note from Geilis called me,
The rest I think you know.

She'd always walked a fine line
Between darkness and the light.
I knew she'd killed her husband
With Cyanide that night.

Nothing to protect her
From the anger of the Laird
Dougal gone to exile – with my Jamie.
I was scared.

The wardens came for both of us,
And Laoghaire came to gloat.
I knew then it wasn't Geilis
Who sent that bloody note.

Tried by the Church as witches,
I knew that we'd be burned.
Ned Gowan did his very best
But then the tables turned.

Burn the Witch, Skelp her!
Take them to pyre.
Burn the Witch, Burn the Witch,
The most painful death is fire.

I will dance upon your ashes,
Laoghaire screamed in glee.
As they flogged me with a strap,
She was all that I could see.

Then through the baying of the crowd,
Cutting like a knife.
I heard my Jamie shouting.
He'd come to claim his wife.

****

Drama in the hall

Come quick lass – your wanted.
Come quick to the hall
Fetch one of your potions
Or – better fetch them all !

Dougal has gone fighting drunk
His wife at home is deid.
On the quiet he blames himself.
He's drunk off his heid.

There was Dougal, sword in hand.
Trashing up the place
Screaming like a banshee.
Tears running down his face.

He'll thrash the ears off anyone
Trying to get near.
Wee Angus was the only one
Not showing any fear.

I loaded up the bottle.
With laudanum ,I think
I'll give it to wee Angus
To try and make him drink.

Wee Angus raised the bottle high
And offered it to his Chief
They drank a toast to Maura
We all sighed with relief.

As the big War Chief Mackenzie
Collapsed upon the floor
And with Clansmen holding arms and legs
Was carried out the door.

Drop him and I'll have yer balls!
The Lairds voice was a warning.
Put the drunken sot to bed
I'll see him in the morning!

****

Fixing the Mill

Little things remembered
Small details in your mind
Things that you can laugh at now
That time has them behind.

The day I went to fix the mill
And redcoats came a riding
One had to be a millers son
And I was in the water hiding.

He came striding to the mill wheel
And gave it a good shake.
I was in the water weed,
Hiding like a snake

I held my breath for ever!
He would not go away.
The cold was doing things to me
I remember to this day.

I pushed the wheel from underneath,
The gears began to bite,
And hung my fathers flannel drawers
On the paddles in full sight

The redcoats rode off on their way.
They'd be back later - maybe
I was in the millpond
As naked as a baby.

As I emerged – granny McNab
Was sitting on the grass
Skirts arranged around her.
Laughing at my arse.

I would have blushed, had I not been blue
I tried to hide my tackle
That rare old crone stared back at me
And then began to cackle.

Young Rabbie to be a stable boy?
She asked in wily tones
Grinning, and her toothless laugh
Shaking her old bones

Claire was sat beside her,
Laughing fit to burst
I'd give grannie anything.
But I'd have my sark back first.

Caught at a disadvantage
She pushed it to the hilt
It's hard not to grant a favour
When she's sitting on yer kilt.

****

Master Raymond

Mysterious French apothecary,
Perceptive and alert
His shop is full of remedies
Though some of them are dirt.

We do not know much of him
Though he moves amongst Royalty
He dabbles in the dark arts
That is the reality.

Mainly he is un demoniste blanc
His powers are for healing
His aura blue, the same as Claire.
They have the same good feeling.

Where he ever came from
We really do not know
Older than very time itself
Traveller ? That may be so.

He saves Claire's life, by laying hands
He brings her out of fever
But then falls foul of St Germaine
The Count is a deceiver.

Before the King, Claire must judge
Who uses those dark powers
By sleight of hand the Master
Puts an end to the Counts hours

Banished then from all of France
He leaves without a trace
Is he in some other time
Travelled to another place

****

Parisian to the core

When I was a still a child
I made a big mistake.
I stole something from a Scotsman
A little wooden snake.

Of very little value
To anyone but him.
I stole it from his sporran
And he didn't feel a thing.

It changed my life forever,
That's when I met milord.
For that is what I called him
When my future he assured.

He took me from the brothel
I was born there, no excuse
And he paid me to steal for him
My talent put to use.

He vowed he would look after me
If I lost a hand,
Or any other body part
In the service of his land.

Now I am married to his daughter
No longer a French rake
Maybe stealing Sawny
Was not such a mistake.

For milord adopted me
When I married Marsali,
Fergus Claudel Fraser.
I have his name and family.

****

Redcoats

We joined the British Army
To serve the King and fight
A soldiers bed and food and clothes
And whores to spend the night,

Garrisoned in Scotland
It's wet, and cold, and bleak.
We cannot even understand
The strange language that they speak.

The men fight hard like savages
Their women are all whores
The children are all bastards
We'll treat them such I'm sure

We are here and at the Kings command
We do not need another reason
To hunt out all the Jacobites
And those disposed to treason.

We take exactly what we want.
And punish who resists
Fight back and we'll flog you,
Hung up by your wrists.

And when we've raped your women.
And stolen everything
Remember that we do it all
In the name of our King.

****

The Laird and his wife

A master politician
A shrewd and careful man,
The undisputed figurehead
Of the Mackenzie Clan.

Not a figure to be crossed
He does not suffer fools.
Is swift to issue punishment
To those who break the rules.

The Clan ,is his priority
Before any other cause.
His men at arms will not be sent
To fight Jacobite wars.

Legs crippled and disjointed
He rarely leaves his lair.
His Brother is his War Chief
At his right hand – ever there.

We see little of Letitia
His feisty red haired wife.
Always in the background
But cutting like a knife.

She is a witch it's rumoured
Is know to have her say.
Keeps Callum always on his toes,
Behind the scenes ye Ken

What goes on behind closed doors,
In public they are one
Letitia has her husbands back.
The power behind the throne.

****

The Bonnie Prince

Charles Edward Stuart!
What were people thinking,
To put you on the Scottish throne
They must have been drinking.

Brought up an Italian
Pampered by the pope.
You'd never been to Scotland.
You never had a hope.

You misled the Highland Clansmen
You misled your own advisors.
An army can't be armed and fed
With money spent like misers.

You thought yourself a leader,
You tried to look the part,
Believed the ones that flattered you,
It was all doomed from the start.

Fortunate in your victories,
Your army gave their all.
The English learned their lessons.
God couldn't stop your fall.

God will not grant you victory,
On that moor so wet and sodden.
God will not save the Scottish Clans
At the Battle of Culloden

* * * *

25

Wedding Planning

Dougal thinks I marry lightly,
Believes it's all on paper.
Just wed her, and then bed her
And if she complains then rape her.

But Claire will be mine forever,
And I tell it true,
I will make this day a special one,
If it's the last thing I ever do.

I rummage in my sporran,
I find a special thing,
The front door key to Lallybroch
That will make a ring.

I marry as a Fraser
I am ready – Je suis prest.
I will marry in my Tartan
Not Mackenzie on this day.

And we will be married by a priest
In the papist way
And in a church – before God
And the blood oath we must say.

My bride must also have a dress,
Something verra fine,
to suit the Lady Lallybroch
That she'll be will be when she is mine.

And so I laid my conditions down,
To wed my Sassenach
A marriage till we both should die
There would be no turning back.

****

Second time Around

It was a formal document
Writ with quill and ink.
Sat on a log I read it.
And took down a stiff drink.

But I already had a husband,
Though he was not yet born
How could I take another one.
Tomorrow in the morn.

The groom did not seem worried
In fact he seemed quite sure.
It didn't seem to phase him.
That I'd done it all before.

I stamped my feet a little.
And had another drink.
I think I drank the bottle
While I had a think.

It wasn't really bigamy
Franks time was not yet due
Was Jamie then, my first husband.
Had he just jumped the queue!

I did get very drunk that day,
I don't remember night.
I woke up with a steaming head.
And looking quite a fright.

But someone had produced a dress
And a very charming ring.
A church bedecked with candles
And a priest to do his thing.

And oh my when I saw the groom
Dressed in highland splendour.
I had a feeling that the wedding night
Would see my heart surrender.

****

A Back wood man from Wales

We meet him first at River Run
A back woods man alright.
With a hairy face and hairy back
He looks a real sight.

A Welshman with a heart of gold
He lives up in the hills.
Trading with the Indians
Using his trapping skills.

A friend of Aunt Jocasta
He knows his way around.
Teaches Ian about the Mohawk tribe
Helps the Frasers find their ground.

Handy with a scrubbing brush,
He gets Rollo smelling sweet
After tangling with that skunk
He scrubbed him up a treat.

We almost lost John Myers
When he tangled with that bear,
Though it was really human
It gave him quite a scare.

Wounded and bedraggled
With a big rip in his Breeches
Don't you worry readers.
Claire will soon have him in stitches.

My Family of Waifs and Strays

Sleep ,tonight a stranger
Demons in my dreams,
I wander through my memory
And try to change the themes.

Thoughts that make me happy,
Make my life fulfilled,
The constants and the anchors
That the demons haven't killed.

My children are a rare mix
Of blood, and waifs and strays
Brianna, is an ocean
And two hundred years away.

Ian, Fergus , Marsali
Have lives now of their own
With weans to look after,
A generation grown.

Joan has her own calling
Life given to the Lord
A kinder lass there never was
To spread the word of God

And wee Faith is not forgotten
I shall always carry blame,
Did my headstrong selfishness
Put you in a grave.

And Willie, 9th Earl Ellesmere
You may deny your sire
Look in the mirror and you'll find
All that Fraser fire.

****

Palmistry

Handed down the generations
A gift, or maybe skill ?
Prophecy, or witchcraft,
Call it what you will.

Everyone is born with lines
Engraved upon their hand.
Does each hidden meaning.
Show your destiny is planned?

The lines which one is born with
Are just a basic outline,
Life will add some twists and turns
As you journey down your timeline.

Some marker posts may be laid out,
You may not choose that highway,
Some detours may be added.
Some lay-bys and some byways.

Your palm is on a journey
It fits you like a glove.
Is it's basic layout planned.
By some power up above?

Is it fate, or is it luck?
A Freeman or a slave,
Is our lifetime all mapped out?
From the cradle to the grave.
****

The Privy Counsel!

How Ian Murray knew me
I really had forgot.
He had remembered everything.
I would rather not.

A teenage boy of privilege
Travelling with papa.
Taken to the back woods.
Sleeping under stars.

Used to getting my own way,
Spoiled and loud and brash.
If Mac the groom had been there
I'm sure my arse he'd thrash.

We called upon the Frasers.
Papa sought to find
The great tall red haired Scotsman.
Who lived inside his mind.

A cabin in the forest
Basic with no frills,
Papa seemed to love it
It just gave me the chills.

My first shock was – that Scotsman
He was Mac the groom.
But he would not recognise me,
When I stepped into the room.

How is he called Fraser now,
How has he a new life.
I did not believe him
When he said he had a wife.

And oh! that evil smelling shed
I'd rather use a pot.
I'd never been in such a thing
And I'd really rather not.

And I fell in that dank dark hole
The contents…….. no mistake.
Covered me from head to foot
And then there was the snake!

Even Papa teased me.
When they pulled my from that place.
And everyone recorded
The look upon my face.

Ian Murray saw it.
And remembered what he saw.
The blazing eyes, the Fraser stare,
His Uncle to the core.

Filthy , stupid, angry
Venomous frustration
Falling in a privy is,
Complete humiliation

****

The first visit

My god the place was so remote
It took an age to find,
A peaceful, ordered visit
Not what we had in mind.

The Laird was plainly not at home,
Greeted by his daughter
A Bonnie girl, with fiery eyes
A lamb come to the slaughter.

Let's have some entertainment.
While the men load up the cart.
Humiliate the lassie
Before we make a start.

He strode into the dooryard
Hate blazed from every pore
Trying to save his sister
Before I hurt her even more.

He was really more my type,
A rare specimen of flesh,
He would be a challenge
And my soul he would enmesh.

Tied up in the gateway
I marked his virgin skin
With intent of further punishment.
That I would soon begin.

She spat at me with venom
She kicked me and she fought,
Then laughed at me, and taunted
She emasculated thought.

Without the stimulus of fear
The screams that will entreat.
The more I tried the more she laughed.
Humiliation was complete

She could not know, that I had planned
A vengeance like no other.
The deepest darkest pit of hell,
Where I would break her brother.

****

Life at Ardsmuir

Herded in like cattle
Many to a cell,
A days hard work on little food
The Scottish form of hell.

Few here with the will to fight,
We were already beaten
Culloden ripped the soul from us.
The bit the rats hadna eaten.

They searched the cells for tartan
A reminder still for some
Stuffed into the cracks in walls.
A tiny scrap of home.

The guards had cause to fear me
I'd been sentenced twice to die.
As murderer and traitor.
Though there were reasons why.

The only man they kept in chains
With nothing left to lose.
I'd kill most of them ,with just one hand.
If my anger was let loose.

Clansmen need a leader,
They found me work to do.
Red Jamie, The Dun Bonnet, gone.
They Christened me Mac Dubh.

So I tried to make things better
To hunt for food and that.
Blankets, greens and medicine
But they didn't want the cat.

So we rebuilt the prison.
And then they moved us on,
Indentured to the colonies
Far away from home.

They would not send me with them
My crimes deserved no quarter.
They paroled me as a servant.
And sent me to Helwater.

"Twas Lord John Grey arranged it
Only later could I tell.
It was a favour to the only friend
The good Lord found in Hell.

****

Thoughts in Print

A day like any other day,
A respectable façade,
A cover for my murky trade
To make detection hard.

The web I weave around myself.
To hold it all together,
Is born of lies and of deceit.
It won't stand much more weather.

I tried to live the settled life
I tried to love another,
Her children are my family,
But I can't live with their mother.

So I open up the print shop
And settle to my work
Pen has more power now than sword.
Print more power than dirk.

Thought nothing of the chiming door
Thought Geordie was returning
Chided him for taking time
My irritation burning.

A voice not heard for twenty years
But still as clear as bells
Spoke from above and put my thoughts
In seven kinds of hells.

That voice ,embodied in a face
And a form not an illusion.
Threw my fragile web of lies
Into a mass confusion.

For twenty years I have not slept,
Without thought of her returning.
For twenty years I kept alive.
Her memory, and the yearning.

And here she is, a real thing
Not seen through a fever.
A living, breathing, solid Claire
Who I have loved forever.

I felt the blood drain from my face,
My legs went weak for sure
The ale pot fell before me,
And beat me to the floor.

How do I start to tell her
Of the mess that is my life,
That in the time she was away
Laoghaire became my wife.

Claire is all for honesty
But I know that I must lie.
God ,I need to hold her tight.
And pray she does not fly

I will tell her bit by bit
Of most that I have done.
The tangle which is now my life
And hope she does not run.

****

Finding Jamie

Frank was dead, and history said
Jamie was alive.
Though he had gone back to die,
He managed to survive.

One officer of Frasers,
Survived that awful day
Was not executed,
Was spirited away.

We tracked him through the records,
And the history books
An outlaw, then a prisoner
indentured to a Duke.

Then lost him in the wilderness
Of him there was no trace.
To be so close, but far away.
Hope had been erased.

A snip of conversation,
A random line of Burns,
A pamphlet in a library file.
On these my future turned.

A printer now in Edinburgh
Still against the Crown.
But I could go back and find him
We had finally tracked him down.

With my affairs in order,
No ties left behind,
Brianna sent me with good grace
Her father, I should find.

And so I reached the print shop
He was standing at the press.
Broad of shoulder, red of hair
I was scared I will confess.

I watched as he went ashen,
And then began to weep,
His legs gave way, quite gracefully
He collapsed into a heap.

We clung on to each other,
Checking both were flesh,
I wept tears of unchained joy
He cried with happiness.

We burned into each other,
How then would we start
To patch a hole two decades wide.
Two lives lived years apart.

He promised to be truthful
I had nothing there to hide.
He told me things in little bits,
Like driftwood on the tide.

In my mind I did the jigsaw
Of the pieces of his life.
I later found he'd missed a piece.
The one which was his wife!

How could I forgive him
This was treachery complete.
That woman tried to have me burned.
A bitch skilled in deceit.

Confronted by his love for me
She shot him in the arm,
It was me that she was aiming for.
But he would not have me harmed.

I listened to him talking,
Could not apply a balm
To never ending grieving,
And a mind he could not calm.

How he tried to live a normal life
he married without thinking.
To please his sister Jenny
He must have done it drinking.

And so we started over.
No longer in our youth.
With a love that's shared when two souls bared.
Agree to tell the truth.

****

A Man of Letters

Need a lawyer! Neds the man
To sort your legal papers
The breadth of his experience
Would give a lady vapours.

A man of education,
By books, and school of life,
From the city to the Highlands,
And he doesn't have a wife!

Qualified in Edinburgh
He is a man of letters,
He also is a Jacobite
Though he's avoided any fetters.

He operates from Leoch
And rides out for the rents
Big buddies with the War Chief!
I think they share a tent!

They have a common purpose
Money for the cause.
Parading Jamie's flogging
To Jacobite applause.

The Lairds rent goes in one bag,
Their collection in another,
They'll be in some hot water,
If it's found by Dougals brother.

Ned will get off lightly,
Talk his way around,
Callum will not banish him,
There are too few lawyers left in town.

So if you need your Will writ,
Or treason is your game,
Sell your house? Divorce your wife?
Ned Gowan is the name !

He'll also source a wedding dress
If you're really stuck.
But don't ask where he found it!
"Twas just a stroke of luck

****

Jenny Murray

My brother came home with a wife
A Sassenach for sure.
He started well, upsetting me.
Calling me a whore.

Of consorting with a redcoat
Of having Black Jacks child
Didn't know I'd married Ian Mor
Thought I'd been defiled.

Strutted back into the house
Saying that I lied
I've been in charge since he ran off
Since our father died.

His wife is quite a strange one
She clearly loves him dear.
But has no family and no history.
I find that really queer.

I will have the truth from him
Before he moves back tween these walls
And if he's telling lies to me
I shall have him by his balls.

Brother or no brother
He need not expect
That strutting in and playing Laird
Will earn him my respect.

I want him to be happy
To settle here with me
Without a price upon his head.
And most of all be free.

There'd been all sorts of stories
Came from Leoch, of his wife.
She'd best not hurt my brother.
For him I'd give my life.

She appeared out of nowhere.
Some believe she is a witch
Others that she is a spy
I will find out which is which

My brother clearly loves her
And I will play along
Until the day she crosses me
And does my brother wrong

****

The Full Scottish

Just to set the scene a bit
I shall start the night before
Jamie spent a cold hard night
Asleep outside my door.

The Inn was full of drunkards
And with my safety on his mind
He feared I might have 'visitors'
Of a most unwelcome kind.

At breakfast in the morning
I was sat amongst the men
Porridge doled out for breakfast
But an atmosphere – ye ken

I don't have much Gaelic
Their signals were quite clear
The rabble making phallic signs
And grinning ear to ear.

Angus slammed his bowl down
Then picked up his dirk,
Rupert drew his breath in.
Murtagh gave a smirk.

Even Ned began to look around
For a convenient place to hide
And Dougal quietly nodded.
At Willie by my side.

Angus growled and strolled across,
Said a few words to the lad.
Rammed his head into his porridge
Called him something really bad.

Bodies crashing everywhere!
Plates and fists were thrown
I sat in the corner.
Puzzled and alone.

Bloody Scots! must they pick
A fight at any chance.
More bodies thrown against the wall.
A stamping, kicking dance.

It ended quick as it began
The losers having fled!
I patched up Mackenzie wounds
Bandaged Mackenzie heads.

As guest of the Mackenzie,
They may insult me to be sure.
But god help any other man
Who calls their guest a whore!

I suppose I must be thankful
That the finest of all forces
My red haired, young protector
Had been sent to feed the horses.

****

A Snake In the Grass

I didn't see it coming,
But an exploding powder keg
Of pain went through my body
Venom flowed into my leg.

My eyes were on the buffalo;
It was a big mistake.
To not look all about me -
I didn't see that snake.

Its poison slowed my senses;
I felt myself go cold.
But my leg was throbbing hot as hell,
Fever taking hold.

I couldn't walk, I couldn't crawl,
Could barely raise my head
If Roger couldn't get me home.
I'd verra soon be dead.

Roger Mac !now is the time
To really show your worth!,
Me dying in the bushes
Is not a time for mirth.

He made me stay quite motionless
He prayed for me a bit.
In English not in Latin
The Presbyterian twit!

He built a sledge of branches,
And dragged me through the wood.
Until they came to look for us,
I didn't think he could.

Roger never gave an inch!
Though I was racked with pain
He cursed me and cajoled me.
As the poison coursed my veins.

Claire was clearly frightened
She wasn't making jokes
Her cheerful bedside manner
A nervous, see through, hoax.

So she filled the hole with maggots,
And made me drink her broth.
She thought I couldn't see the saw
She hid under the cloth.

I'd rather die a whole man
Than live with half a leg
She'll not touch me with that saw.
No matter how she begs.

She could not inject me,
For lack of a syringe.
My arse was safe from needles,
Though the maggots made me cringe.

Stubborn and rebellious
I'd die a proper man
With two whole legs, and all my bits.
At least that was the plan.

And I'd die in my own bed
With my wife beside me.
I'm going out a happy man,
With God alone to guide me.

A determined woman is my wife
I turned back from the light
When she said she needed me
That's when I chose life.

And my daughter's swift invention
Came neatly to the pass
Though I'd rather Claire jabbed a needle
Than that snakes fang in my arse.

****

Burying Hayes

Hayes was dead, I saw him hanged
At his last he saw a friend,
So full up wi whisky
He didna feel the end.

A superstitious bugger
He feared the dark at best
The churchyard was the proper place
To lay his bones to rest.

We gave him a fair send off
In the Gaelic sung some songs
With his body in the wagon
Left Charleston to the throngs.

The Priest had wanted paying,
Of flesh he'd have his pound,
To rest a sinner like old Hayes
In consecrated ground.

'Twas dusk when we left Charleston
A shovel had been bought.
We picked a spot beside the wall.
That Hayes would like, we thought.

He was hiding in my wagon,
Still fettered up for hanging,
Scairt Young Ian witless,
When his chains they started clanging.

He talked the talk, he was a thief
But a friend of Hayes, ye ken
Condemned to hang for smuggling.
And I was taken in.

By candle light we dug Hayes grave,
We didn't tell the priest,
Buried him and said a prayer.
At rest now at least,

Hayes now safely in the ground
We must resume our journey,
The wagon should be empty now
Not acting as a gurney.

He talked me into freeing him,
I would not hand him in,
Shook my hand and thanked me.
And parted with a grin.

I miss judged that Irish bastard,
With his easy line in charm.
I should have seen it in his eyes
He only meant us harm.

****

Robbed

All aboard the Sally Anne,
We headed up the river,
Despite the lack of any waves,
Jamie's insides were aquiver.

All of our belongings
Were loaded on this boat,
Nothing else here to our name,
I hope we stay afloat.

The river seems so peaceful
Lush ground on either side,
All of mother nature
Undisturbed, as on we glide.

A beautiful and wild land,
Where anyone may roam,
Four travellers and a half wolf dog,
Looking for a home.

At dusk ,we tied up for the night.
We thought it safe from harm,
Twas Rollos growl and barking
Sounded the alarm.

They stormed the cabin in a mob
Even Jamie could not fight
Knife to his throat, four pinned him down,
Struggle as he might.

They knew we had some money,
They searched him to his skin
Found what they were looking for,
And then did not give in.

What they did not take they broke,
My surgeons kit and things
The leader of these vile men
Tried to steal my rings.

I took them off quite gracefully
And held them in his sight
Then rammed them hard into my mouth.
And swallowed them in fright.

I felt hand between my teeth
His fingers on my tongue,
He made me spit the rings back out
But I had swallowed one.

The one he stole meant all to me
But wasn't worth a lot.
Twas the Iron one, from Jamie
From the key to Lallybroch.

I recognised that Irish brogue
His voice an evil sonnet,
I would not forget that night
At the hands of Stephen Bonnet

We arrived at Aunt Jocastas,
With nothing to our name.
But the clothes that we stood up in,
And the will to start again.

****

Kidnapped

Young Ian swam to silkie isle
For the contents of the box
I saw him through the spyglass
Climbing up the rocks

Hid behind the island
Sails unfurled in the lee
A foreign ship ! what brought it here?
With a flag of Portuguese.

Ian thrown into the boat
Like a bag of bones.
That was what they'd come for
The gold and precious stones

We watched helpless from the headland
As she sailed off to the west
Destined for some foreign land
With Young Ian as a guest.

The clansman said that gold was cursed
Protected by the witch
Belonged to the Mackenzie
And she would return for it.

My blood ran cold, at my next step
To follow across the sea,
To rescue Ian and send him home,
From wherever he may be.

A ship from cousin Jared,
A cargo for Jamaica.
For that was where that ship was bound,
And we must overtake her.

I swallowed hard, my stomach turned.
Could I stay alive,
For three months on a pitching deck
Spewing o'er the side.

****

Goats and Hell

Josiah told us where it was,
The cabin in the wood
It stank of goat, it stank of hell
It stank of nothing good.

Dark and uninviting,
How could anyone survive
In a rundown hovel in the trees.
Was anyone alive.

Ahoy the house, we called out,
Jamie held the gun.
No answer, was there no one there,
Had everybody run.

A face came to the window,
Threatening but afraid,
A woman, worn by hardship
From the righteous path had strayed.

To buy the twins their freedom,
The reason for this call.
What was in this house of horrors,
Really capped it all.

She had tortured old man Beardsley,
Just keeping him alive,
Enough to let him feel the pain.
Of burns he could survive.

He must have been a cruel man
Death would be a blessing,
I left that one to Jamie,
With my oath I'll not be messing.

Oh God, Mrs Beardsley,
My grin is not of mirth,
Her waters have just broken,
The woman's giving birth !!

She did not take her baby,
When she left at dead of night
She found the Twins indentures,
And was gone before the light.

Wrapped up with her Indian child,
The deeds to Beardsleys land,
Someone would find a home for her,
With inheritance, understand.

We buried old man Beardsley
Underneath a tree,
Alongside all his other wives,
I think I counted three.

We took the rest to Brownsville,
The baby and the goat
The hungry mite, foraging
Down the front of my old coat.

I often think of Fanny,
For that is what they called her,
When we left her there in Brownsville,
As their adopted daughter.

****

The White Sow

She was the dearest piglet,
Wriggly and pink.
But always up to mischief,
She quickly learned to think.

We kept her longer than we should,
For we were quite mistaken,
That she would join our family.
That pig should have been bacon.

A streak of independence.
Every day she would escape,
Leaving a trail of destruction.
And carnage in her wake.

The list of things she's eaten
Is getting quite impressive
Jamie's hat, Briannas drawers,
That pig gets more aggressive.

Growing bigger every day,
Now with piglets of her own,
She got to choose just where she went.
Or her wrath would soon be known.

She does exactly as she likes,
She scares the pants of men,
No amount of food enticement
Will keep her in a pen.

Even the Indians respect her.
The white sow from the ridge,
I'm sure she'd have been bacon.
If we'd only had a fridge.

****

Birthday Checklist

Ten toes, two feet
Two legs - that's neat
Nearly lost one of those.

Fingers – nine
But that's just fine,
If the rest work – I suppose.

Two arms to hold the one I love,
One heart – still beating- strong

One chest – where someone's head can rest.
To check the heart has not gone wrong.

Two eyes – to see the whole of you
Not quite so sharp this year.

Two ears – to hear you laughing
A sound I love to hear

One nose to hold the scent of you
Two lips to tell you that........

The best bit is all working fine ....
Happy Birthday Sassenach!

****

****

Part 2

I have Included in part two , poems which I have written on other subjects, Most of them before I became Outlander Obsessed. But it shows I do think about other things.

Welcome to Part two.

Hope you enjoy as much as you have enjoyed the rest.

Watching the Rugby (Wales v Scotland)

Yesterday was Saturday
In Wales we watched the game.
Scotland up in Murrayfield
A match that's never tame.

A nail biting first half
Scotland 9 points ahead
Wales will have their work cut out
Come on the men in red.

Watching on the pod cast
I recognise that man
It's John Quincy Myers
Ah ..... so that's how they got Sam.

Half time we get Sam on
Gloating quite a bit.
He's wearing Heughan no 10
He likes his Scottish Kit.

My husband has me rumbled.
Pod cast ! he says ,that's new
You've only got that thing on
Because he's in Outlander too.

Shut up and watch the rugby
It's getting quite exciting
They must have had a row at half time.
Wales have come out fighting.

My daughter tells me to calm down
I'm shouting at the screen
Mum the ref can't hear you!
And your language is obscene!

Wales won! We can't believe it.
But only by one point.
I'd love to see Sam Heughans face
Do Scottish disappointed

Come to Wales next year,
Will we see you in the crowd.
Best you bring your ear plugs
The Welsh can cheer quite loud.

****

Domestic Update

Here's a little update
On the course of my affliction.
I wake up thinking Gaelic
And talk in Scottish diction!

I tried to swap the duvet
For some sheepskins and a quilt.
And keep a blade under the mattress
Where I can reach the hilt.

My hubby looks like Dougal
He's bald and wears a beard.
But his humour is like Rupert,
This makes life pretty weird.

I know he's planning something
I can read his heid.
He's scouring the free ads.
For a coat of red.

He's learned to fire a musket,
The lessons were quite odd
He doesn't quite know what to do,
With that great rammrod.

He talks a lot, of powder,
And a lot, of balls (he talks a lot of it anyway)
There's a five foot Brown Bess musket,
Propped up in my hall

We've had a lot of rain in Wales,
The garden is quite sodden.
Has he asked some friends round.
To re-enact Culloden?

****

Turning Leaves

The leaves are turning
The old men say,
A sign that Autumn is on her way.
The trees will shed their summer clothes
And dress themselves in brown and gold.

The wind will come and strip them so
Their leaves will fall and lie below,
Become a carpet on the ground
Where hiding conkers can be found.

When winter comes the trees are bare,
The cold gives them no clothes to share,
They go to sleep until the Spring
Wakes them – to bring the green again.

And winter may bring in the snow,
More often rain as we all know.
Time to get the woolies out,
Wrap warm when you go out .

And on those lovely cold crisp days
Watch your breath cloud in a haze,
Hear your feet crunch in the frost
While the sleeping spring remains quite lost.

But all of life is waiting there
For warmth to bring them to the air.
The colour will return in spring
And make amends for everything.

The year will start its self you'll see,
The leaves will bud upon the tree,
The bulbs will push their coloured treat,
Through the frost beneath your feet.

Written - 8 Sep 2020

Flashback

Last night I had a Flashback,
I have them more and more.
I'm banging hard on walls of steel
I'm pinned down on the floor.
I'm screaming for the love of god
Please help me,
Let me go
My all is pleading let me out!
The answer - always – no!

I'm half asleep
My body shakes,
I'm like a dog half dreaming.
I wake up scared
In total dark - my inner senses screaming.
My family sleeps - unaware
My thoughts are in a race.
I lie awake and type my dream to try and find
A place,
For all the pain my mind endures in nighttime's darkest place.

I'm quiet now
My mind is still
My thoughts are dark and deep
A silent tear runs down my face
Please god give me sleep.

Written - 10 Jun 2020

Gone Missing

The slamming door
The walk away,
That is the hardest part.
Shutting out the ones you loved
Never looking back.
The longer gone ,the harder
To turn and make amends
Time increases distance
Silence never bends.
And when you finish walking
What have you got to show
For all those miles
You put between
You and those you know.
Existing in a twilight world
Where bonds are easy broken,
A cardboard bed
On cold hard stone
A sleep with one eye open.
They will always look for you,
They will not sleep at night,
They imagine you are coming back
To make their old age light,
With each new town,
With each wet day,
Their hope is slowly fading.
That you could walk back to their life
Without your freedom trading.
So turn around
Swallow your pride

Before it starts to snow.
A sleeping bag,
A cardboard box,
Is all you have to show.
Words will fade just as your eyes
No longer bright with hope,
The worn out look,
The endless tired,
The alcohol and dope,
They wanted all the best for you,
Through you they lived their lives,
The weight of expectation
Was always in your mind.
The fear of always failing,
Of letting family down.
No smiles for you at bedtime,
Always a dark frown.
They miss you now for what you were,
The brightest and the best.
Go home to them,
Give back their hopes,
Then everyone can rest.

Written - 20 Jun 2020

Black Lives Matter

Black Lives Matter!
Sure they do,
They matter to us all.
But so does this old land of ours
We cannot watch it fall.

Our land is rich in history,
It's the stuff that make us Great,
United by a common goal
To fight to stamp out hate.

This land has seen much fighting,
It's seen some civil wars,
Britannia ruled not only waves
It ruled on distant shores.

And for all the good and bad she did,
She will look after you,
Not judge the colour of your skin
Whatever is it's hue.

And now we fight on three home fronts
Some things are not our battle
The right , the left, the virus
Protesters sabres rattle.

Each one is determined,
fighting for their cause
But quietly destroying,
This land – mine and yours.

Boarding up our hero's,
Disregarding law,
Take a breath and think it out
What are you fighting for?

Peace?
Harmony?
Equality?
Your country warts and all?
Fight in one direction
Or everything will fall.

A country fair to everyone,
A country not despised,
A country who's rich history,
Has not been sanitised.

Written - 14 Jun 2020

Lockdown Revisited

It's grey outside,
It's raining,
The trees are waving too,
Dropping leaves like litter,
As we enter lockdown two.
It's rained all week,
It's autumn.
It rains this time of year,
I don't mind walking in the rain
But it's getting worse I fear.
People walk like zombies,
Staring at the floor,
Dogs sniff by with sodden coats,
They like the rain I'm sure.
A muffled up good morning.
Smothered in a mask.
Shoulders hunched against the wind
A walk is now a task.
I walk for several hours,
Clocking up the miles,
Passing grunting walkers,
Nobody ever smiles.
This awful autumn lockdown
Has made the people sad.
Please let us out for Christmas
Before we all go mad.

Statues and Statutes

In towns and cities they look down
In bronze and marble silence,
Hero's, villains, pioneers
Defaced by acts of violence.

In marble nooks and leafy parks
Remembering deeds once done,
Men and women from the past
Who's relevance is gone.

Still they tell a story,
Remind us of a time
Of wars , of battles and empires
Of good deeds done and crimes.

Is it right to tear them down ?
Perpetuate unrest,
Or learn from their dark history
Not just pick the best.

We cannot re write history,
Only educate,
The generation growing up
Teach them not to hate.

Don't destroy the world around you,
Don't tear down all the good,
Learn from all that's gone before.
Treat humans as you should .

Before you throw that bottle!
Before you aim that gun!
Think of the damage you may cause,
That cannot be undone.

****

When your you isn't you anymore.

It's hard to admit when you aren't right.
When the you ,you knew has left.
It may be gone just for a while -
but you will be bereft.

Hands reach out to stop your fall,
Their help may be rejected.
You are not ready for their aid
Your you is too dejected.

Your sadness fills each waking hour,
Grief fills every minute.
The cruelty of human beings
pushed you to your limit.

You say you'll take the help they give,
To keep the helpers happy -
but the you ,you knew
Which isn't there
won't accept what's in it.

So for a while you won't be you,
And others must accept it.
Your you will heal itself in time,
Time heals all things, doesn't it?

You will return to your right place
That will not be too long,
And when your you comes fighting back,
It will be twice as strong.

I promise.

Written – 28th August 2019

****

Turning Corners

The road of life is winding,
It bends and twists each day.
You rarely get a straight bit
To help to smooth your way.

These curves are there to test us,
They make us question why,
We can't see round the corner
See the hill we have to climb.

Learn to read the traffic signs,
Watch for signs of danger,
Then to the winding bends and hills
You will not be a stranger.

You cannot see the future,
You don't know where your road ends
And trying to predict it,
Will drive you round that bend.

All life is for a reason
You may not know it yet.
And the light after the darkness
Is the happiest you get.

Is life one big circle ?
Is that what we've found?
Can we avoid the darker bits
Next time they come round ?

Life's lessons are for learning,
Take them to your heart.
Recognise the bad bits,
And avoid them from the start.

****

Circles

It's amazing how the world turns
And all things run in rings.
Conversations circle
The round of life still brings.
Endless variations
On the day before,
If every day was all the same
Then life would be a bore

Each day is an adventure,
You can't predict it's flow,
Try as you may
You cannot say
how your day will go.

The good days
And the bad ones,
The happy and the sad,
Days you wish had not begun
And ones you wish won't end.

Does each person have a book
In which their life is told.
Some are long and some are short
Not destined to get old.

The intertwining stories
Which weave our day to day,
Play out in an endless scene
Of humanities great play.

The actors start from nothing
They develop with the play,
Even the stars go back to ashes
On their dying day.

****

Walking Home from Nights

Familiar places,
Empty streets,
Puddles wet
Below my feet.
All is quiet,
All is dark,
Except beneath
The streetlights arc.
The sun is just about to rise,
It climbs it's stair,
Into the skies.
I won't see it at its heights
Today – as I walk home
From nights.
Work bag
slung upon my back,
Along the path and cycle track
Up the path
Into my house.
Up the stairs creep,
Like a mouse
Draw the bedroom curtains tight
Shut the door – keep out the light
Set the alarm
So I can say
I didn't miss all this summers day.

****

Dunraven Bay

Sitting on the cliff top
I stare out at the sea,
Today it's calm
It soothes my mind,
I don't need company
I can see forever
Stretching in the sun
Seagulls gliding on the breeze
Soaring, having fun.
The grassy slope
The crumbly cliff
The pebble beach below
Today there is a gentle breeze
And not a whiff of snow.
Yesterday was different.
The tide was in a rip
Waves threw their temper on the beach
The pebbles start to slip.
Wind howled across the cliff top
It was not safe to climb
White peaks topped the angry sea,
With fronds of whipped up brine
Carved between the hillsides
Life could be far away.
On my cliff of solitude
At Dunraven Bay.

Turning Out

He hears the gate drag on the stones
His pushes at the door.
His ears twitch,
His feet all itch,
He stamps and snorts and paws.
Barely contained excitement
Oozes from his skin.
Take these rugs off!
Let me out.
His patience wearing thin.
He's been in for the winter,
He's had his fill of oats,
It's time for rest and lush green grass
For shedding winter coat.
Straining on the lead rein,
Desperate for release,
To explode in frantic energy,
And then to roll in peace.
To dig his shoulder in the mud
To fling his legs about.
Winters gone and Spring has come
It's time to turn him out

****

American Scrapbook

We found the old brown suitcase ,hidden in the trash,
It's contents were beyond repair
Black with damp and ash.
They my mothers story lived out in the war
With clippings in a scrap book, of all the things she saw.

At fourteen she was sent away to live across the sea,
With classmates from her school, they sailed,
To foster families.
They risked the ocean crossing – the trip across the pond
To avoid the coming war – when London would be bombed

Evacuated from our land to the USA,
She landed there exactly on her 15th Birthday.
Boston Massachusetts, would be her second home,
Welcomed there with open arms
But sent there all alone.

The scrapbook tells of parties, and Christmases and dances
There are letters there from those at home
Teenage first romances.
Summer camp and skiing,
She learned to shoot a rifle,
Our mother was a sure shot
With her you did not trifle.

Letters from an airman,
Training as a nurse,
A busy life – a social whirl
But homesickness a curse.

Despite impending danger
She felt the need to roam,
The bit firmly between her teeth
She booked her passage home.

Back to war torn England,
She knew she would not fail,
Finished off her training
Became a Nightingale.

Her life was never boring,
Never keeping still
Our mother was a live-wire
Even when she was ill.

When we found the scrapbook
Her life was nearly through,
We read to her, her memories
From clippings fixed with glue.

Pointing at one picture
A name came to her lips,
She smiled and started laughing
At schoolgirls in gym slips.

Her ancient face was grinning
She chuckled on and on,
We will never know just what
Barbara might have done.

Written - 28 May 2020

Parents

We are parents,
So we nag you!
We feel it is our job.
To make you tidy up your stuff
And not live like a slob.

We are parents,
You are our pride and joy!
Our love is always there,
When times are tough
When life is rough
We are the ones who care.

This year has been a strange one,
For us as well as you.
And though there's only three of us
I'm sure we will get through.

You were blessed with may gifts
And that is not a rumour.
Thank god you got your mothers brain
And fathers sense of humour.

Have a very happy birthday,
As you look forward to.
A lifetime of adventure
I'm sure you'll have a few.

And don't forget your parents
When you fly the nest.
Look at all their attributes
And take away the best.

****

The clock in the Hall

Standing tall and strong of oak,
It ticked the pass of time.
Passed down generations
To the female line.
It ticked and tocked in my Great Aunts house
And on the quarter it would chime.

The chimes were bright and cheery,
It sang a merry song.
And after every four short chimes
It's Baritone would Bong.

I would go and wind it
And polish up the face,
With it moon and stars engraving
And clouds with sun to chase.

I stood on the piano stool,
And turned the winding key
To put the weights back at the top
Every Saturday at three .

Winding done we'd sit and talk
And I'd wait for the bus,
She'd cut the cake – home made of course
No 'bought cake' there for us.

We looked forward to these visits
When she would tell me tales,
Of family from long ago
Her family from Wales.

When my great aunt passed away
The clock went slightly mad.
It bonged thirteen at midnight
It's big brass face looked sad.

Passed on to my Sister she didn't have the space
For a big old clock with a
Big oak heart and a shiny big brass face.

So the clock went to my mother
He stood proudly in her hall.
And once again he ticked and tocked
And kept the time for all.

We came along and fixed his bong
And kept his insides working,
Mum cleaned his face and polished him
Her duster never shirking.

He kept the time for forty years ,standing by her door
As he kept it in my Great Aunts house
For sixty years before.
His ticking was the heartbeat, that welcomed us all home
His chiming was the merry tune, that said you weren't alone.

My mother sadly passed away,
The clock ticked on and on.
He stood there in the empty hall
His family all gone.

We packed up all the furniture,
China packed in cases,
We sorted through the pictures,
Of long forgotten faces.

He ticked on, he kept the time
Until he had to stop.
The day my mother's house died,
When my sister took the clock.

And when I finally locked the door,
My last look round was done,
I knew I had no time left there,
Because the clock had gone.

****

The Authors Wish

I got on the rollercoaster
And somebody pressed start,
My hobby to be put to use,
My poems are not art.

Wordsworth was a poet
A proper one, and Keats.
I write rhymes that fill my head.
Sometimes they come out sweet.

If I could have one thing
Before I go to glory.
I'd like to hear Sam Heughan
Read 'Bedtime Stories'

It's never going to happen,
I doubt he'll read my book
But if it turns up on YouTube
Perhaps you'll take a look

And tell me !!

© maggiej2021

Made in the USA
Middletown, DE
28 February 2021